ler's
ns wear
LOW
LOW
LOW
PRICES
120

image

www.manofaction.tv

XXV

JOE CASEY WRITER
IAN MACEWAN ARTIST

BRAD SIMPSON COLORIST
SONIA HARRIS GRAPHIC DESIGNER
RUS WOOTON LETTERER

CHAPTER ONE

WHEN WE TOUCH, GIVE ME SUCH A FUNNY FEELING IN MY BRAIN
I'M SO POSSESSED BY YOUR LOVE, SOMETIMES I DON'T EVEN KNOW MY NAME

ON AIR
BOOM-BOOM, KIDDIES! THE RED LIGHT IS ON AND THAT MEANS THE SUN BEGONE! YES, WE'RE KICKIN' OFF THE NIGHT SHIFT NICE AND SMOOTH!
ALL YOU CREATURES OF THE DARK, ALL YOU BOPPERS ON PATROL, ALL YOU DAY-SLEEPERS... I AM RIBBED FOR YOUR PLEASURE!
SO IF YOU'VE GOT YOUR EARS ON OUT THERE, THEN YOU KNOW YOU'VE GOT PREFECT PATTERSON RIDIN' THE MIC, THE VOICE OF WMAK FM --
DUFFY
BROADWAY
TIMES
W46
ONE WAY
ONE WAY
ONE WAY
NO TURNS
-- THE PREFECT WAY TO SPEND A PREFECT NIGHT!
FIVE
Sightseeing TOURS
NATURE'S OWN PAPAYA REVITALIZER
GIRAUDS
TAXI!
GOTTA GET TO RYDERS ALLEY.
KIND OF IN A HURRY...
I HEAR YOU LOUD AND CLEAR, MAN...
CLICK
ROCKWELL CO.
FARE
TRUNKS 50 CENTS EACH
... WE'RE ON OUR WAY.

I'M 'BOUT TO SPIN SOME KOOL & THE GANG FOR YA'... AND THE O'JAYS AFTER THAT...
BUT FIRST --
-- THOSE OF YOU THAT TURN YOUR DIAL TO WMAK EVERY NIGHT KNOW THAT I'M YOUR EYE IN THE SKY, WATCHIN' OUT FOR EACH AND EVERY ONE OF YOU.
IT CAN BE A WEIRD WORLD WHEN THE MOON IS UP...
...YOU NEVER KNOW WHAT YOU MIGHT FIND OUT THERE...
HUH.
WELL, HE AIN'T LYING...
... THIS COULD BE ONE OF THOSE NIGHTS.
HEY, MAN. I DON'T WANT TO SCARE YOU BACK THERE.
BUT IT LOOKS LIKE SOMEONE DON'T WANNA LET US PASS...
... JUST HOLD ON.
WH- WHU...?
WHAT'RE YOU --

ROOAARRR
AUUUGGHHH--!
CALM DOWN.
JUST ONE OF THE HAZARDS OF THE JOB --
SKREEEEEE

OKAY, LEMME JUST TAKE CARE OF THIS.
WHATEVER YOU DO...
... DON'T GET OUT.
YOU NINJA CREEPERS CAN BE A PAIN IN MY ASS, Y'KNOW THAT...?
LUCKILY, I GOT EXACTLY WHAT YOU NEED...
... SO LET'S DANCE.

... ON THE MEAN STREETS OF THIS CITY -- IT'S EVERY MAN FOR HIMSELF! EVERY SHADOW IS FULL OF WEIRDNESS AND MYSTERY! WATCH OUT FOR THEM BLACK CATS, Y'DIG?
SO, IN THAT SPIRIT, GONNA SPIN A LITTLE "SUPERSTITION" FROM MY MAN, STEVIE...!

YOU'VE STILL GOT YOUR SKILLS --
-- BUT NOT NEARLY ENOUGH TO SAVE YOU FROM THE INEVITABLE, LITTLE PAMELA...
AIN'T SO LITTLE ANYMORE. YOU JOKERS KEEP TAKING YOUR SHOTS -- AND KEEP MISSING THE TARGET.
I'M STILL HERE. AND I'M GONNA BE FOR AS LONG AS I WANT.
YOU BRAVADO IS PATHETIC! HAVE YOU SO EASILY FORGOTTEN THE FORCES ALIGNED AGAINST YOU?!
SOON, IT'LL BE ENTIRE ARMIES OF DARKNESS THAT RISE UP TO SMITE YOU LIKE THE MALCONTENT YOU ARE!
PERSONALLY, I CAN'T WAIT TO SEE YOU BURN!
WHATEVER.
SHORK
IS...
... IS IT OVER...?
PRETTY MUCH.

AT LEAST FOR NOW.
KTHUNK
KTHONK
KTHUNK
... NEED A STIFF GODDAMN DRINK AFTER ALL THAT...!
HEY, MISTER...
... YOU OWE ME FIVE-FIFTY.
DON'T WORRY. I DIDN'T CHARGE YOU FOR THE LITTLE DETOUR BACK THERE...
SURE, SURE...
... JUST TAKE IT.
DRUGS
PRESCRIPTIONS
COSMETICS
KTHUNK
KTHONK
KTHUNK

... AS THE SUN BURNS BRIGHT ONCE AGAIN, THIS IS PREFECT PATTERSON -- THE VOICE OF WMAK -- SURRENDERING TO MORNING DRIVE TIME.
KEEP IT TOGETHER, BABIES. UNTIL THE NIGHT SHIFT BEGINS AGAIN...
BEAR CAB
CAB CO.
HIRE A CAR!
KTHU
EVANS!
ARE YOU CRAZY?!
GRIZZLY.
YOU REALLY WANT ME TO ANSWER THAT...?
DON'T GIMME NO LIP NOW!
DISPATCH TELLS ME YOU CALLED IN WHAT YOU SAY IS A "MINOR TRAFFIC ALTERCATION" --
-- AND YOU ROLL UP IN THIS?!
WHAT'S THIS SUPPOSED TO BE -- SOME KINDA MODERN ART?!
AND THE PROBLEM IS...?
THE PROBLEM IS -- YOU MANGLED YOUR RIDE!
YOU AIN'T SUCH A HOTSHOT CABBIE THAT YOU CAN DO WHATEVER YOU WANT OUT THERE AND GO TRASHIN' MY CARS...!
I'M SURE IT'LL BUFF RIGHT OUT.

YOU *KNOW* I'M THE BEST YOU GOT.
MAKE SURE THERE'S A NEW RIDE READY FOR MY SHIFT TONIGHT, 'KAY...?
DAMMIT, EVANS--!
CAN'T GET ENOUGH
PREFECT.
WHAT'S SHAKIN', BABY DOLL?
YOU'RE A LITTLE LATE GETTIN' HERE. EVERYTHING GOOD...?

C'MON, PAMELA... DON'T GIMME *THAT.*
SOMETHING HAPPEN OUT ON THE ROAD...?

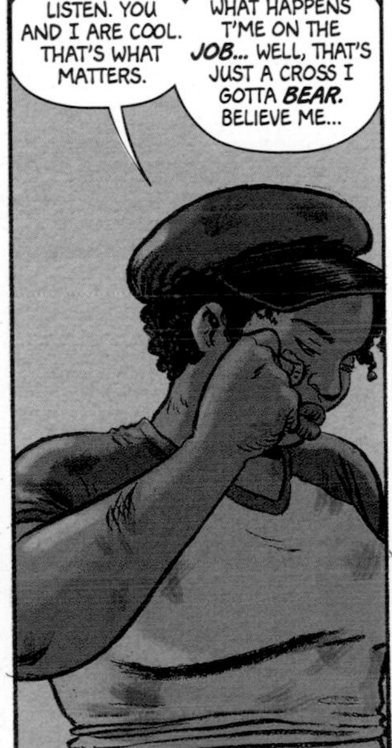
LISTEN. YOU AND I ARE COOL. THAT'S WHAT MATTERS.
WHAT HAPPENS T'ME ON THE *JOB...* WELL, THAT'S JUST A CROSS I GOTTA *BEAR.* BELIEVE ME...

... IT'S NOT WORTH *TALKIN'* ABOUT.
IF YOU *SAY* SO.
'SCUSE ME IF I DON'T COMPLETELY *BUY* THAT RAP.

OH, NO? YOU NEED SOME CONVINCING?
YOU BETCHA. UP CLOSE AND PERSONAL --
SO YOU GONNA MUSCLE ME NOW? SHOW ME WHAT'S WHAT?
Y'KNOW, IF I DIDN'T KNOW BETTER... I'D THINK YOU WERE TRYING TO DISTRACT ME.
LIKE YOU DON'T WAN GET INTO THE REA NITTY-GRITTY SO YOU THIS TRIP ON ME INSTEAD.
NO TRIP. YOU'RE MY MAN. WE'VE BOTH BEEN WORKIN' ALL NIGHT...
... IT'S TIME RECONNE Y'DIG?
AW, HELL...

TAKE A GOOD LONG LOOK. TRY AND MEMORIZE EVERY STREET, EVERY ALLEYWAY, EVERY NOOK AND CRANNY...
RE DAMN SURE GONNA HAT KNOWLEDGE WHEN E DRIVING YER BEAT, LIL' LEADBELLY.
WHY YOU KEEP CALLIN' ME THAT?
I DUNNO. SEEMED APPROPRIATE FROM THE DAY I STARTED RAISIN' YOU.
WHATEVER. JUST GET ME BEHIND THE WHEEL.
GET ME A FARE. GIMME AN ADDRESS --
PAMELA EVANS: THE GREATEST CABBIE THERE EVER WAS!
-- I'M GONNA TEAR IT UP OUT THERE!
THIS IS AN HONORABLE PROFESSION, YOU UNDERSTAND. YOU MIGHT BE A GREEN PEA NOW, BUT I WANT YOU ACTING LIKE A VETERAN.
NO SMUGGLING. NO STRETCHING YER HOOD. WE GOT A CODE AND YOU LIVE BY IT.
YOU JUST WATCH. GONNA MAKE YOU PROUD, DAMOCLES...!
I ALREADY AM, GIRL.

OOOHHHH--!
THIS IS GONNA BE SO COOL! THANK YOU SO MUCH FOR TEACHIN' ME!
THIS IS EXACTLY WHERE I BELONG, DAMOCLES!
WITH YOU. DOING THIS.
IT'S ALL I'VE EVER WANTED TO --
HOLD ON, LIL' LEADBELLY...
... THINK WE MIGHT HAVE A SITUATION HERE.
?
WHAT... WHAT'S GOIN' ON...?
WELL, I DON'T KNOW IF I COULD SAY FOR SURE, BUT I CAN SAY THIS...

... LOOKS LIKE TROUBLE.
ON'T WORRY, DAMOCLES!
THIS IS THE *OTHER* THING I'M PRETTY GREAT AT!
PAMELA, *WAIT* --
-- NO!
NO!
PANT!
PANT!
PANT!

SIGH
DAMN...!
THE
THE PROMISCUOUS
EXTRA
IN COLO
STRANGER
FILMS
PREMIERE
SEX
WIFE
DIXIE
HOTEL

WHERE'RE YOU HEADED, MA'AM...?
WEST NINETY-FOURTH AND LEXINGTON, PLEASE.
AND *DON'T* CUT THROUGH THE PARK.

YOU GOT IT.
YOU MIND IF I TURN ON THE **RADIO...?**
-- THE GREAT BEN E. KING AND **"SUPERNATURAL THING."**
THAT'S **PART ONE,** BY THE WAY...
PEAKING OF THE **UPERNATURAL,** OKS LIKE WE GOT **FULL MOON** OUT TONIGHT.
NOW DON'T YOU GET SPOOKED. THAT'S WHEN THE **NIGHT SHIFT** REALLY TAKES OFF!
C'MON. WOULD **PREFECT PATTERSON** STEER YOU WRONG--?
HOLD UP, BABIES. GOTTA **STREET BULLETIN** HERE... HOT OFF THE WIRE...
E BREAKING NEWS FOR O-NOCTURNALS. A LITTLE **IGHT MADNESS** GOIN' WN RIGHT NOW OUT THERE.
YOU KNOW HOW IT **IS...** SOMETIMES NATURE HAS A WAY OF **WORKING THINGS OUT** --
-- BUT YOU **DON'T** WANNA GET CAUGHT UP IN THE **MIDDLE** OF IT.
COULD GET A LITTLE **HAIRY,** MY BABIES...
NO SHIT.

84 ST
3 AV
ONE WAY

UMMM...
... M-MAYBE WE ***COULD*** CUT THROUGH THE PARK...?

TOO LATE FOR THAT.
SORRY FOR THE DELAY, BUT I NEED TO GET INTO THIS...

DON'T YOU WORRY. I'M NOT ***DEFENSELESS.***
MA'AM, I'M ONLY GOING TO SAY THIS ***ONCE...***

DO NOT.
GET OUT.
OF THIS CAB.

... SOME PEEPS ON THE SCENE ARE CONFIRMING THE *PLAYERS* INVOLVED...
... THE *MORNINGSIDE HOOLIGANS* AND THE *MG ARZACHS* ARE IN HEAVY NEGOTIATIONS, SO FOR ALL YOU LAW-ABIDING *CIVILIANS* OUT THERE TONIGHT --
-- TRY AND *STEER CLEAR* UNTIL THINGS ARE GOOD AND *SETTLED.*
'SCUSE ME...
... NEED TO *BORROW* YOU FOR A SEC.

NG--!

THAT'S IT...

WAIT...
FZZZ

... YOU GUYS AREN'T MONSTERS.

JUST *ASSHOLES.*

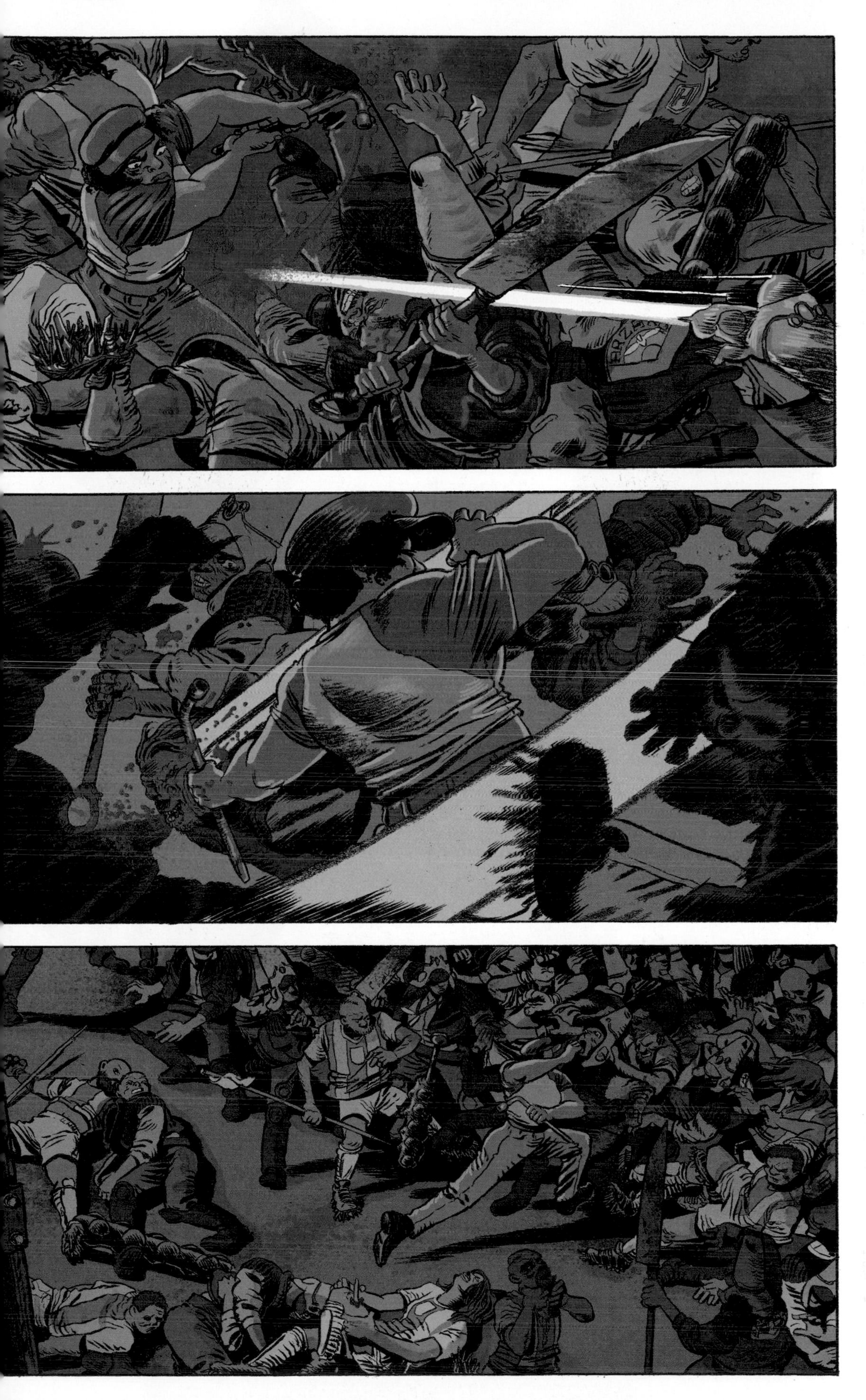

WHAT... IN THE HELL...?!
UHHH...

-- YOU'D BETTER GET BACK HERE!
?

DID YOU THINK WE WOULD NOT FIND YOU, EVANS-CHILD? YOU AND YOUR SMUG MOUTH?!
YOU TOOK FLIGHT BEFORE YOU COULD WIN THE WAR --
-- NOW YOU PAY THE PRICE FOR YOUR UNDYING INSOLENCE!

KING
STING

CHAPTER TWO
MCMLXXV

IT'S NOT LOVE I'M RUNNING FROM, IT'S THE HEARTBREAK I KNOW WILL COME...

THIRTEEN YEARS PREVIOUS:
PAMELA EVANS! YOU MUST BE CRAZY--!
JUST LAY BACK, DAMOCLES --
-- I'M FOUR FARES IN! SMOOTH SAILING ALL THE WAY!
YOU THINK TAKING ONE OF MY CARS WITHOUT PERMISSION IS "SMOOTH SAILING"?! LEMME TELL YOU SOMETHING, LIL' LEADBELLY --
-- IT AIN'T SMOOTH FROM WHERE I'M SITTING! AND THAT HAPPENS TO BE DEAD CENTER IN THE DISPATCHER CAGE! YOU HEAR ME?!
YOU MAY BE THE HIPPEST THIRTEEN-YEAR-OLD ON THE BLOCK, BUT THAT DON'T MEAN THAT I'LL PUT MY REP ON THE LINE!
YOUR "REP"?! GIMME A BREAK!
I DON'T NEED NO BACK TALK --
HOLD UP.
SOMETHING FUNNY GOIN' ON UP AHEAD...

THIS SURE AIN'T NATURAL, IS IT...?
NYYAH--!
WHA--? HEY, JERK-OFF --

OH DAMN...!

NO --
-- NO!
GAH--!
STOP--!

NGG--!

Can you FEEL it? She possesses a deep and infinite FIRE...
... that will serve her well in the perils to come.
Indeed. She will make a worthy COMBATANT...
... once she is properly GROOMED, of course.
Seconded.
No doubt she will be an avatar of our righteous FURY.
She will cut a wide swath of destruction through ALL our enemies' territories.
She will bring forth a final --
OKAY.
I DUNNO WHERE I AM... OR WHO THE HELL YOU THINK YOU'RE TALKIN' TO...
... BUT I AIN'T NOBODY'S "AVATAR."
Ignorant whelp. Clearly you are not FIT to comprehend the JOURNEY you are about to embark upon.
We shall ADD to your fire --

-- with some of our OWN.
That was merely the FIRST step to total acclimation.
With the right WEAPON, any war can be WON, fellow travelers...
... especially when WE will control the weapon.
We shall bring ORDER to these dark, lawless realms.
Let us further PREPARE this one to be the instrument we need...
... forever locked in immortal SERVITUDE.

EVEN IN THE DEPTHS OF THE UNDERWORLD, THERE IS NO SWEETER TASTE...
... THAN THAT OF PURE REVENGE.
WOULDN'T YOU AGREE, EVANS-CHILD?
I SHOULD'VE WIPED OUT YOUR TRIBE WHEN I HAD THE CHANCE...
... NOW ALL THIS SHOWBOATIN' IS GONNA COST YOU.
THIS REALM STINKS OF CORRUPTION -- EVEN WORSE THAN ANY REALM IN THE WAR-TORN REGIONS OF DOOM!
I THINK I'M GOING TO ENJOY MY
-- AND YOUR DEATH WILL BE MY FIRST WICKED DELIGHT!
ON
OKAY, BABIES! 'RE STILL LIVE AND RIC WITH PREFECT TERSON ON YOUR RUE SOUL STATION -- WMAK FM!
LOOKS LIKE THAT HEADS-UP BETWEEN THE HOOLIGANS AND THE ARZACHS HAS RAMPED UP INTO SOMETHING A WHOLE LOT WILDER...
... KEEP YOUR WITS ABOUT YOU OUT THERE, NIGHT PEOPLE! YOU DON'T WANNA END UP GETTING RACKED...!

HUHHNNGG--!
AHHHH, THAT FELT GOOD!
THEY MIGHT' TRAINED WELL
-- BUT NOT WELL ENOUGH, EH?!
ANOTHER SLAVE TO THE GRIND --
-- LET HER DIE LIKE ONE!

PUNK-ASS BITCHES--!
TEN UP! E GETTIN' 'E STREET L EVERY INUTE!
LIKE PERS VIN' TURF ASY!
TIME TO STEP UP, JACKOS!
YEAH! NO MONGREL-MOUTHED HORROR SHOW IS GONNA UPSTAGE OUR ASPHALT AUTHORITY!
MORE DERANGED DENIZENS?! THIS WILL TAKE BUT A MOMENT --
-- JUST A BROKEN HEARTBEAT!
HEY, SCUMMY --
-- WHADDA YOU KNOW FROM HEART?
YOU EVEN HAVE ONE INSIDE THAT ROTTED CARCASS?!
TELL YOU WHAT --

-- LET'S FIND OUT!
Her will is STRONG. Her compulsion to WIN is FIERCE.
Endless hordes has she vanquished in this controlled environment. It has become a TIRESOME exercise.
Then do we all agree that she requires no more PREPARATION...?
We do.
Let her now venture forth into the SHADOW TERRITORIES on our behalf to perform a horrible BLITZKRIEG...
GET IT IN GEAR, NIGHT PEOPLE! IT'S AN URBAN JUNGLE OUT THERE!
IT'S ONE OR THE OTHER, Y'DIG --
-- KILL OR BE KILLED!
I CAN TASTE YOUR FEAR ON MY TONGUE, EVANS-CHILD.

BONG
DON'T --
-- CALL ME THAT!
YESSSSSS...
... YOUR IRON SERVES AS A BEACON THAT DRAWS ME TO YOU... I REMEMBER WELL THE TASTE OF IT --
-- BUT DO YOU REMEMBER THIS?!
GYUUHH--!
HA!
DESPERATION BRINGS ONLY DEATH --
-- AND HERE IT IS!

HOW FITTING THAT YOU MEET YOUR END RIGHT HERE -- ON YOUR HOMELAND!
I'LL DRAG YOUR BONES BACK WITH ME -- AFTER I'VE PICKED THEM CLEAN, OF COURSE!
DON'T WORRY. I'LL DO IT SLOW...
YOU TALK TOO MUCH --
GRRAAAAAA-

URK--!

YOU THINK... THIS LONELY VICTORY... **ENDS** THINGS...?
AKK--!
YOU KNOW... THERE WILL COME... MANY **MORE**...
...

CLANG

YEAH...
... I'LL BET.

RESPECT.
NO DOUBT.

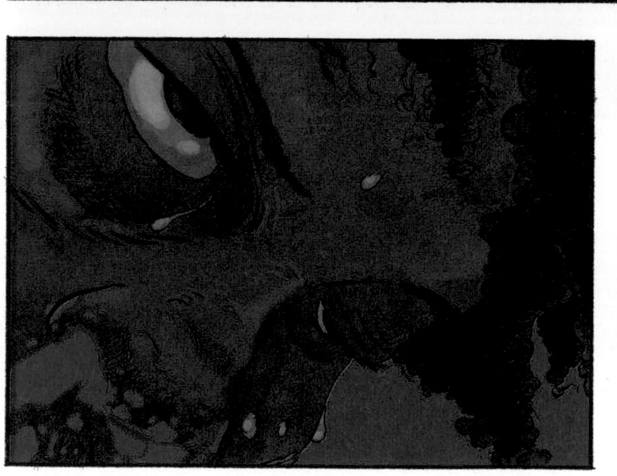

PREFECT...

OWNHALL
coltrane
HYDROGEN PEROXIDE
... NNNN...
FINALLY AWAKE, HUH...?
YOU'RE PRETTY MESSED UP... AND I'M NO DOCTOR...
... THINK MAYBE I NEED TO SCOOT YOU OVER TO THE ER, Y'KNOW...?
... NNNNO... NO HOSPITAL...
... I'LL HEAL...
... JUST NEED A LITTLE TIME...
YOU'LL HEAL? ALL ON YOUR OWN? I DON'T GET IT...
... UMMM, YOU WANNA MAYBE LET GO OF THE TIRE IRON, GIRL...?
HELL NO.

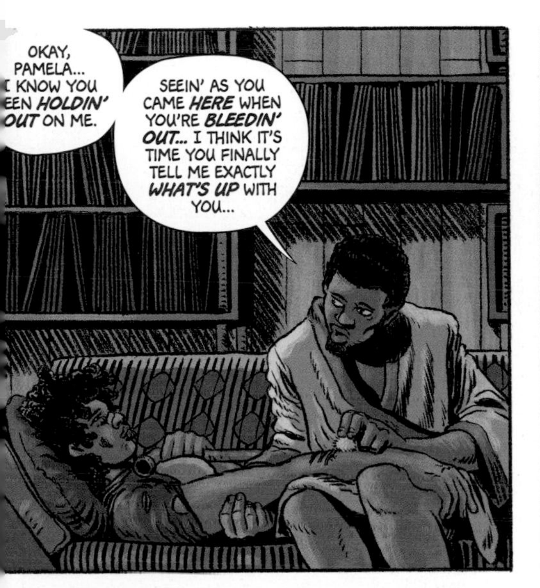
OKAY, PAMELA... I KNOW YOU BEEN HOLDIN' OUT ON ME.
SEEIN' AS YOU CAME HERE WHEN YOU'RE BLEEDIN' OUT... I THINK IT'S TIME YOU FINALLY TELL ME EXACTLY WHAT'S UP WITH YOU...

WHAT'S UP WITH ME? BABY... SOMETIMES I DON'T EVEN BELIEVE IT...
BUT THERE'S A PLACE THAT EXISTS... FAR OUT FROM HERE... I WAS TAKEN THERE AGAINST MY WILL TO FIGHT THEIR WARS FOR THEM...
SO, FOR A WHILE, I DID...

IF YOU HAVE COME HERE SEEKING DEATH, EVANS-CHILD --

-- REST ASSURED, YOU HAVE FOUND IT.
YOU WILL NEED MORE THAN A HEAVY REPUTATION TO WITHSTAND OUR FIERY RANKS.
THE SEETHING HORDES OF MUSPELLEGRA DO NOT ACCEPT INVASION LIGHTLY.

I... I DON'T GET IT.
THEY... THEY TOOK YOU? AND TO DO WHAT?! AND WHO --
I... SERVED MYSTERIOUS MASTERS...
... AND I SURE MADE ME SOME ENEMIES FIGHTIN' COUNTLESS TURF WARS.
BUT NOT THE KIND YOU THINK...
GRRAAAA--
THIS IS WHAT WAR FEELS LIKE, EVANS-CHILD!
NO QUARTER ASKED --
-- AND NONE WAS EVER GIVEN.
MY REALITY... HAD SHIFTED...

... AND ***THIS*** PLACE WAS A REALM OF SHADOWS AND DEATH AND ALL KINDS OF ***WEIRDNESS.*** REMEMBER THE ***BEDTIME STORIES*** WE WERE TOLD AS KIDS? I'M TALKIN' ABOUT THE REAL ***SCARY*** ONES... THAT'S THE KIND OF WEIRDNESS I WAS UP AGAINST. AND IT WAS ALL ***REAL.***

BUT I'D BEEN WELL TRAINED. I COULD ***FIGHT.*** I COULD ***WIN.*** I WAS ABLE TO TAKE WHATEVER ***FEAR*** I HAD AND ***USE*** IT. I WAS SENT INTO TERRITORY AFTER TERRITORY... I WAS A ***FIRST-STRIKE WEAPON*** AND I DID MY JOB LIKE A PRO. AND PRETTY SOON I HAD A HEAVY ***REP.***

I DID SERIOUS ***DAMAGE*** TO EVERY TRIBE I WOULD RUMBLE WITH. THEY CALLED ME *"EVANS-CHILD"* TO TRY AND PSYCH ME OUT. BUT IT NEVER WORKED. AND I LET THOSE BURNOUTS THAT THOUGHT THEY ***OWNED*** ME BELIEVE I'D FIGHT FOR THEM ***FOREVER...***

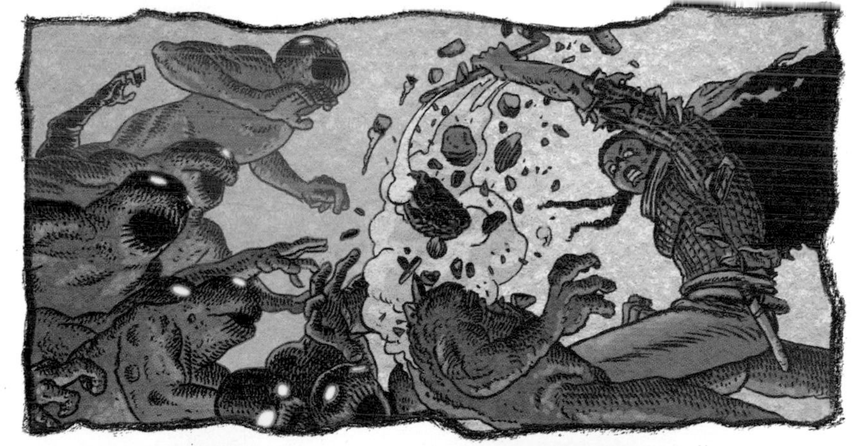

. EVEN GH I HAD OWN GENDA.
BUT THAT WAS MY LIFE... I DIDN'T KNOW HOW LONG I WAS TRAPPED THERE...
S-SO, OKAY... WHEN YOU WERE A KID, YOU GOT KIDNAPPED AND SHIPPED OFF TO... WHAT, THE UNDERWORLD...?
DAMN, GIRL.

DEMONS... MONSTERS... WALKING NIGHTMARES... I TOOK 'EM ALL ON BEFORE I MANAGED TO GET MYSELF BACK HERE.
BUT THEY NEVER FORGOT. AND NOW...

... THEY'RE COMIN' FOR ME.
JEEZUS-
MY VINYL--!
AIN'T YOU FREAKS GOT NO RESPECT FOR A MAN'S MUSIC TASTES?!
WAIT --

JUST KEEP CHILLIN', BABY DOLL -- I AIN'T LETTIN' NO ONE GET TO YOU!
FECT!
ON'T--!
I GOTTA. YOU AIN'T IN NO CONDITION--!
SO LET'S SEE WHO'S UP IN HERE READY TO BUMP UGLIES WITH ME!
THIZZZ -- IZZZZ -- IT!
I ZZZEE THE EVANZZZ-CHILD LIEZZZ BEFORE UZZZ --
-- NOW LET NOTHING ZZZTAND IN OUR WAY!
HUURGLLL--!

KOOL GANG
THAT'ZZZ ONE BAG OF FLESZZZ DIZZZPOZZZED OF...
... NOW IT'ZZZ YOUR TURN, EVANZZZ-CHILD...!

MCMLXXV

CHAPTER THREE

HOW DOEZZZ IT FEEL, EVANZZZ-CHILD --
-- TO ZZZZEE HIZZZ BLOOD ZZZPILT RIGHT IN FRONT OF YOU?!
ZZZZUCH A PITIFUL --
YOU... FREAKS --
-- YOU MURDERED MY MAN!
LOOK HOW SLOWLY SHE MOVES!
SHE IS WEAK!
AN EASY TARGET!

HUHHNTT--!
SO VERY SATISFYING, ISN'T IT?!
TO THINK, THE ONCE-GREAT WARRIOR... REDUCED TO SLOBBERING OVER SOME MEAT PUPPET...

.. SOON HIS FLESH WILL ROT INTO THE SOIL OF THIS ACIDIC REALM!
PREFECT...
... BABY...

EVANS-CHILD!
STAND UP AND FACE YOUR DEATH!

RIGHT.

Sketches of Spain
HAYES

YOU WANT IT --
-- YOU GOT IT!
YYEEAAWWWGGG--
I-I FEEL... A BURNING DEEP WITHIN...
TELL ME ABOUT IT.
GONNA GET WORSE BEFOR IT GETS BETTER --
-- I'M PUSHING IT TO BLOW, Y'DIG?!

=KAFF!=
=CHOKE!=
THERE!
ZZZHE MEANZZZ TO TAKE THE FIGHT OUTZZZIDE!
THIZZZ ENTIRE ALM WILL BURN ONCE WE'VE ZZKINNED HER BONEZZZ--!
WAIT! NO --
-- ZZZHE HAZZZ EZZZCAPED!
ZZZUMMON THE HORDEZZZ OF EACH OF OUR HELLZZZ!
WE ZZZHALL FIND HER -- AND DEZZZTROY HER EN MAZZZE!
I COULDN'T *PROTECT* YOU, PREFECT...

... NOW I'M ALL **ALONE.**
AGAIN.
STORY OF MY LIFE.
SO NOW YOU'RE **WORM FOOD,** AND I WONDER WHY I EVEN BOTHERED BOPPING MY WAY **BACK** HERE FROM THE PITS OF DECAY...!
AND I NEVER GOT TO TELL YOU HOW I **DID** IT...
... WITH EACH WAR I **FOUGHT** DOWN THERE, I'D CATCH MORE AND MORE **KNOW-HOW** OF WHERE I WAS AND HOW TO MAKE MY WAY **THROUGH** IT.
FINALLY, ON ONE OF TH MANY BATTLEFIELDS, I HEARD THE WORDS I'D BEEN **WAITING** TO HEAR
... THAT THERE WAS A WAY **OUT.**
AN OLD **MAXIMAGE** HOLED UP ON THE FLIP-SIDE OF THE STYGIAN DUST GLACIERS. I'D GOTTEN THE SKINNY ON HER EXISTENCE DURING A PARTICULAR **RUMBLE** ON THE OUTER REACHES...
... ONE THAT I DIDN'T THINK I WAS COMIN' **BACK** FROM.

IEN ATTEMPTING TO
OOGIE ACROSS THOSE
YING STYGIAN FIELDS
WHILE I WAS STILL
LIN' WAS A JIVE ACT...
... I DON'T KNOW HOW THE HELL I MADE IT.
LET US GAZE UPON THIS SAD THING LAID AT OUR DOORSTEP...
... WE SMELL THE STENCH OF WAR ALL OVER HER.
A WAR SHE WAS NEVER MEANT TO FIGHT.
CURIOUS.
ALL THE WHISPERS I'D HEARD WHILE STUCK IN COMBAT SERVITUDE... THEY'D ALL POUND THE NOTION THAT THIS WASN'T JUST A SINGLE BEING WITH SOME HEAVY MAGICAL MOJO, BUT A LIVING SUMMATION OF GENERATIONS OF SORCERER POWER...
... BUT, TO TELL YOU THE TRUTH, I COULDA CARED LESS ABOUT ANY OF THAT.
I JUST KNEW I HAD TO GET MY ASS BACK HOME.
... NNNN...
... I CAME HERE... LOOKIN' FOR YOU...
... Y-YOU GOT THE POWER TO... TO...
SPEAK TO US NOT OF POWER, CHILD.

WE CAN SMELL YOUR DESIRE. YOU DON'T BELONG HERE, DO YOU...?
YOU POSSESS TOO MUCH HEART TO REMAIN TRAPPED IN THIS AMORAL WASTELAND...
... AND YOUR THOUGHTS ARE NEVER FAR FROM THOSE WHO CONNECT YOU TO YOUR TRUE HOMELAND.
LIKE I TOLD YOU BEFORE... I KNEW THEY'D COME AFTER ME.
THEY STARTED PUNCHING THROUGH A LITTLE AT A TIME. BUT NOW THEY'RE HERE IN FULL FORCE. SO I NEED TO PREPARE.
THIS IS THE WAR I SHOULD BE FIGHTING...
... FIGURE I OWE IT TO THOSE WHO SACRIFICED SO MUCH TO BRING ME BACK.
WE HAVE POKED A HOLE INTO THE OTHER SIDE... WE HAVE FOUND YOUR GREATEST TOUCHSTONE...
... DO NOT BE AFRAID. YOUR TRUE JOURNEY BEGINS NOW.
I HAD NO IDE WHAT SHE WA YAPPIN' ABOUT

-- BUT I'LL BE DAMNED IF SOMETHING DIDN'T GET AHOLD OF ME...!
FOR ONCE IN YOUR YOUNG LIFE... YOU MUST NOT FIGHT. YOU MUST NOT RESIST.
FOR THE REST OF YOUR DAYS, WAR CHILD, YOU MUST REMAIN EVER VIGILANT...
... BUT FOR NOW... GIVE YOURSELF OVER TO THAT WHICH IS MOST IMPORTANT --
-- LOVE.
YOU ALWAYS SAID I WASN'T A TOUCHY-FEELY KINDA GIRL.
BUT THAT'S ME. ALWAYS HAS BEEN.
I JUST GET ON WITH MY BUSINESS.
THAT'S WHAT I WAS TAUGHT FROM THE TIME I WAS ORPHANED... AND HE TOOK ME IN --
-- DAMOCLES.
I GOTCHA, LIL' LEADBELLY!
YOU BEEN GONE WAY TOO LONG --

-- AND I AIN'T LETTIN' YOU GO!
THE OLD WITCH CALLED IT, ALRIGHT. UNTIL YOU CAME ALONG...

... HIS WAS THE ONLY LOVE I'D EVER KNOWN.

TH-THAT'S IT... I CAN FEEL YOU...
... TRYIN' TO CLAW YOUR WAY BACK...

SOMETHING ELSE HE TAUGHT ME...
... IF YOU GOTTA FIGHT, ALWAYS FIGHT TO WIN. EVEN IF YOU DROP DEAD DOIN' IT.

GYYAAHH--!
UHHFF!

JEEZUS... DAMOCLES...
... Y-YOU SAVED ME... YOU PULLED ME THROUGH...
... AAHHH... NNGGG...
... M-MY... HEART...
WHA--? NO...!
PLEASE DON'T DIE... PLEASE...
IT'S... HNG ... OKAY, GIRL...
... IT WAS... WORTH IT...
... JUST GET YERSELF... BACK BEHIND THE WHEEL...
... THAT'S... WHERE YOU BELONG...
A FEW MINUTES LATER, HE WAS GONE...
... SEEMS I'M ALWAYS LOSING THE FOLKS WHO MEAN THE MOST TO ME.
BUT NOW I OWE A DEBT. TO DAMOCLES...
... TO YOU, PREFECT...
... I OWE IT TO BOTH OF YOU...
... TO MAKE DAMN SURE YOU DIDN'T DIE FOR NOTHING.

3 STORES
S. BECKENSTEIN
WORLD'S LARGEST SELECTION
Adler's
men's wear

HEY!
WHO'S IN MY WAREHOUSE--?!

EH...?
WHAT THE HELL IS --
CHILL OUT, GRIZZLY. NOW AIN'T THE TIME.

GAH!
DAMN! 'BOUT JUMPED OUT OF MY OWN SKIN!
EVANS! IS THAT YOU?! WHADDYA THINK YOU'RE DOIN' HERE?!

JUST NEEDED ME A NEW RIDE, THAT'S ALL.

A NEW RIDE?! ARE YOU KIDDING ME?!
THIS AIN'T YER PERSONAL CLOSET, Y'KNOW! YOU JUST CAN'T COME IN HERE AND TAKE WHATEVER YOU WANT!
YOU LOOKIN' TO GET CANNED?!
YOU THINK I CARE ABOUT THIS JOB...?!

U GOT IDEA, YA?!
JUST SHUT YER TRAP AND CONSIDER THIS YOUR MEAGER CONTRIBUTION TO THE WAR I'M GONNA BE WAGING!
WH-WHU... WHAT'RE YOU TALKIN' ABOUT --
DON'T SWEAT IT, GRIZZLY. I'M THE ONLY ONE WHO KNOWS WHAT'S COMIN' ANYWAY.
RIGHT NOW IT'S JUST ME VERSUS THEM -- AND THERE'S AN ARMY OF THEM!
SO I'M GONNA NEED AN ARMY OF MY OWN...
... BECAUSE THESE STREETS ARE YOURS, SUKKAS! HOW MANY OF YOU HAVE FOUGHT FOR 'EM?! BLED FOR 'EM?! DIED FOR 'EM?!
ANY OF YOU WANNA GIVE 'EM OVER TO THE HOUNDS OF HELL?!
'COURSE YOU DON'T! SO YOU GOTTA KNOW THAT THIS IS ABOUT MORE THAN JUST YOUR LITTLE PIECE OF TURF!
A LOT MORE!
I'M TALKIN' TO ALL THE OUTFITS! FROM THE ARZACHS TO THE ARISTOCRATS TO THE HOOLIGANS TO THE DIAMOND DOGS...
SAPPHIRE
STOMPERS

... AND I NEED YOU SAPPHIRE STOMPERS, TOO! IT'S TIME FOR A TEMPORARY TRUCE!
FOR YEARS, I'VE WATCHED YOU WARRING WITH EACH OTHER! AND FOR WHAT?! FOR BRAGGIN' RIGHTS?! GIMME A BREAK!
YOU SOLDIERS WANNA THROW DOWN?!
LEMME GIVE YOU A REAL WAR! AND NOT JUST WITH OTHER BOPPERS SPORTIN' THEIR COLORS...
... THESE THINGS AIN'T EVEN HUMAN! THEY'RE BEYOND YOUR WORST NIGHTMARES!
YOU THINK YOU LIVE IN THE SHADOWS -- THESE MONSTROSITIES EAT DARKNESS FOR BREAKFAST!
SO ARE YOU GONNA LAY DOWN IN FRONT OF THESE BASTARDS?!
OR ARE YOU GONNA SET ASIDE YOUR DIFFERENCES AND FIGHT -- NOT JUST FOR YOUR SURVIVAL... BUT FOR THE FATE OF THE ENTIRE CITY?!
NO MATTER WHAT YOU DECIDE, IT'S STILL HAPPENING! SOME OF YOU HAVE SEEN IT WITH YOUR OWN EYES -- THEY'RE HERE ALREADY!
SO GET YOUR ASSES IN GEAR! CALL IN YOUR AFFILIATES! I NEED YOU LOUD AND PROUD!
I'LL FIGHT 'EM ON MY OWN, IF I HAVE TO... BUT IT REALLY ONLY WORKS IF WE DO IT TOGETHER!
I'M TELLIN' ALLA YOU --
-- THIS IS
RUMBLE
YOUR LIV
SUKKAS

COHEN'S OPTI
SOL M

ONE WAY
NO STANDING
WHERE IS SHE?!
I WANT THE SEVERED HEAD OF THE EVANS-CHILD--!
YES! USE IT AS A PUNCH-BOWL!

ONE WAY
WE'RE GONNA SPILL YER BLOOD IN THE STREETS OF YER BIRTH!
AN ORGY OF MERRY MAYHEM--!

DELANCEY
ORCHARD
FINALLY WE GET OURS BACK!
REVENGE ON THE EVANS-CHILD --
YOU WANT HER --

-- YOU GOTTA DO THE DANCE WITH *US* FIRST!

FLESHBAGS!
SCUMSUKKAS--!

NIKOPOLS

THE MEATY VERMIN ARE TENACIOUS--!
NO MATTER! WHERE IS THE EVANS-CHILD?!
RIGHT HERE, SUKKA.

BOSTON
AWWW YEAH!
YA LIKE A THAT-

GUT CHECK ZZQUADRON!
ZZZZPIT YOUR FIERY NHOLINEZZZ UPON HER!
THAT'ZZZ IT! BULLZZZEYE!
HNNG!
DAMMIT --

HER CHARIOT IS CRIPPLED! NOW IS THE TIME!
LET'S DRAG HER FROM THE WRECKAGE AND TURN HER INSIDE OUT!
YEAH, RIGHT.
Y'KNOW, I WHUPPED YOUR ASSES BEFORE... THINK I CAN'T DO IT AGAIN?
YOU WERE AN INVADER OF OUR REALMS!
HOW DOES IT FEEL TO HAVE THE TABLES TURNED?!

I DON'T KNOW WHAT YOU'RE ON ABOUT. FEELS GODDAMN GREAT.
SEE, I GOT THE HOME-FIELD ADVANTAGE NOW. NOT TO MENTION, I'M PACKIN' SERIOUS HEAT --

-- SO COME ON WITH IT!

I'LL SEND YOU ALL STRAIGHT BACK TO HELL!
DON'T YOU GET IT?! I DON'T WANNA DO THIS!
I'M STUCK HERE!
I'M SICK OF FIGHTING!
I JUST WANNA GO HOME!
EVANZZZ-CHILD --
-- I CAN ZZZTILL TAZZZTE THE BLOOD OF YOUR BELOVED ON MY CLAWZZZ!
I PROMIZZZED YOU WOULD BE NEXT!

YOUR DEATH WILL BE LOW AND ZZZLOW!
YEAH?! WELL, YOUR TRASH TALK SUCKS--!
NUH-UH! YOU AIN'T GETTIN' YOUR JAWS ON ME--!
I WILL ZZZWALLOW YOUR ZZZOUL!
LEMME SHOW YOU HOW WE DO THINGS DOWNTOWN--
RELENT... RELENT...
YOUR RUTHLEZZZNEZZZ... HAZZZ N-NOT DULLED, EVANZZZ-CHILD...

... BUT YOU... ARE ONLY F-FOOLING YOURZZZELF...!
YOU KNOW... THIZZZ WAZZZ JUZZZT... THE OPENING ZZZALVO OF... THE GREATER WAR BETWEEN UZZZ --
-- *
YEAH...
... I KNOW.

... ONE MONTH AGO TONIGHT, WE LOST OUR VERY OWN **PREFECT PATTERSON.** HE WAS LONG CONSIDERED THE VOICE OF **WMAK FM,** AND WE **STILL** MISS HIS SMOOTH SOUL STYLE.
SO THIS IS A SPECIAL DEDICATION. AS THE **NIGHT SHIFT** ARRIVES ONCE AGAIN, GOOD OL' HAROLD MELVIN TELLS US TO "WAKE UP EVERYBODY"...

... THIS ONE'S FOR YOU, PREFECT.
APOLLO
DELFONICS
KOOL & GANG ★ LOVE
NAT TURNER UNLIMITED
HARLEM EM
TAXI!
RIGHT HERE!

APO
DEL
KOOL & G
NAT TU

GOIN' TO BOWERY AND EAST SECOND STREET...
... HOW QUICK CAN YOU **GET** US THERE?

QUICK ENOUGH. IF YOU DON'T MIND CRUISIN' THROUGH A FEW **ROUGH AREAS,** THAT IS.
BUT DON'T SWEAT IT. IF SOMETHING **SERIOUS** GOES DOWN...
65¢ 1ST 1/6 MILE

... I CAN HANDLE IT.
KOOL & THE GANG
NAT TURNER
KING
DONUTS
R.P'S
BOSS

PINUP GALLERY

TAXI
DUSTIN
WEAVER

New-York
MCMLXXV

1975

OTHER WORKS BY JOE CASEY

CODEFLESH WITH CHARLIE ADLARD

ROCK BOTTOM WITH CHARLIE ADLARD

KRASH BASTARDS WITH AXEL 13

NIXON'S PALS WITH CHRIS BURNHAM

OFFICER DOWNE WITH CHRIS BURNHAM

CHARLATAN BALL WITH ANDY SURIANO

DOC BIZARRE, M.D. WITH ANDY SURIANO

THE MILKMAN MURDERS WITH STEVE PARKHOUSE

FULL MOON FEVER WITH CALEB GERARD/DAMIAN COUCEIRO

BUTCHER BAKER THE RIGHTEOUS MAKER WITH MIKE HUDDLESTON

THE BOUNCE WITH DAVID MESSINA & SONIA HARRIS

GØDLAND WITH TOM SCIOLI

VALHALLA MAD WITH PAUL MAYBURY

ANNUAL WITH UKE PARKER, SONIA HARRIS & VARIOUS

NEW LIEUTENANTS OF METAL WITH ULISES FARINAS

SEX WITH PIOTR KOWALSKI

ESUSFREAK WITH BENJAMIN MARRA

ONE WAY
DELANCEY ST
ORCHARD ST
SYRUP
FIGS
OPTICIANS

ler's
wear
LOW
LOW
LOW
PRICES
120

ONE WAY
DELANCEY ST
ORCHARD ST
SYRUP OF FIGS
MOSCOT
OPTICIANS
1 HOUR SERVIC